SPORT BIKES

Katharine Bailey

CRABTREE PUBLISHING COMPANY
www.crabtreebooks.com

Crabtree Publishing Company
www.crabtreebooks.com

To Jim Doyle and the Cablevue team:
thanks for the amazing opportunities.

Coordinating editor: Ellen Rodger
Series Editor: Rachel Eagen
Editors: Carrie Gleason, Adrianna Morganelli,
L. Michelle Nielsen, Jennifer Lackey
Design and production coordinator: Rosie Gowsell
Cover design, layout and production assistance: Samara Parent
Art direction: Rob MacGregor
Scanning technician: Arlene Arch
Photo research: Allison Napier
Prepress technician: Nancy Johnson

Consultants: Petrina Gentile Zucco, Automotive Journalist,
The Globe and Mail

Cover: A modern sport bike takes a high speed corner with
the rider's knee touching the ground.

Title page: A freestyle motocross rider flies through the air after
taking off from a jump ramp.

Photo Credits: Owe Andersson/Alamy: p. 27 (top); Kurt Banks/Alamy:
p. 16; David Bowman/Alamy p. 15; Dominic Burke/Alamy: p. 17;
Michael Juno/Alamy: p. 25; Bjorn Larsen/Alamy: p. 28; Stephen
Olner/Alamy: p. 27 (bottom); Picturesbyrob/Alamy: p. 13 (both); Vic
Pigula/Alamy: p. 29 (bottom); Vario images GmbH & Co.KG/Alamy: p.
26; Adam Ward/Alamy: pp. 8-9; AP/Wide World Photos: p. 11, p. 12, p.
13 (both), p. 14, p. 18, p. 19, p. 21, p. 22, p. 29 (top); AP Photo/Greg
Baker: p. 29 (top); AP Photo/Martiin Cleaver: p. 13 (top); AP
Photo/Martin Meissner: p. 19; AP Photo/EFE, Jaro Munoz: p. 14; AP
Photo/Douglas C. Pizac: p. 13 (bottom); AP Photo/Pascal Rondeau/Presse
Sports: p. 21; AP Photo/Eckard Schulz: p. 18; AP Photo/Paul White: p.
22; Slim Aarons/Getty Images: p. 30; Franco Origlia/Getty Images: p. 31;
Ron Kimball/Ron Kimball Stock: p. 5 (bottom); National Motor
Museum/Topham-HIP/The Image Works: p. 14; Manchester Daily
Express/SSPL/The Image Works: p. 7; SSPL/The Image Works: p. 6. Sean
Nel/istockinternational: cover; Other images from stock CD.

Library and Archives Canada Cataloguing in Publication

Bailey, Katharine, 1980-
   Sport bikes / Katharine Bailey.

(Automania!)
Includes index.
ISBN 978-0-7787-3013-2 (bound)
ISBN 978-0-7787-3035-4 (pbk.)

   1. Motorcycles, Racing--Juvenile literature. 2. Motorcycles--
Juvenile literature. I. Title. II. Series.

TL440.15.B33 2007   j629.227'5   C2007-900649-3

Library of Congress Cataloging-in-Publication Data

Bailey, Katharine, 1980-
   Sport bikes / written by Katharine Bailey.
      p. cm. -- (Automania!)
Includes index.
ISBN-13: 978-0-7787-3013-2 (rlb)
ISBN-10: 0-7787-3013-1 (rlb)
ISBN-13: 978-0-7787-3035-4 (pb)
ISBN-10: 0-7787-3035-2 (pb)
   1. Motorcycles, Racing--Juvenile literature. I. Title. II. Series.

TL440.15.B352 2007
796.7'5--dc22   2007002917
                                       LC

Crabtree Publishing Company
www.crabtreebooks.com   1-800-387-7650

Printed in the U.S.A./092015/CG20150812

Published in Canada
Crabtree Publishing
616 Welland Ave.
St. Catharines, ON
L2M 5V6

Published in the United States
Crabtree Publishing
PMB 59051
350 Fifth Avenue, 59th Floor
New York, New York 10118

Published in the United Kingdom
Crabtree Publishing
Maritime House
Basin Road North, Hove
BN41 1WR

Published in Australia
Crabtree Publishing
3 Charles Street
Coburg North
VIC, 3058

Contents

Good Sports!

Sport bikes are some of the most exciting motorcycles in the world. They are built to win races and perform on all different types of terrain. Some roar around pavement tracks at top speed while others launch off jumps and fly through the air.

Winning on Two Wheels

Sport bikes are built for racing in competitions. There are many different kinds of sport bikes and each type of bike is built for different sporting events. A road-racing machine is built to reach top speeds on a **tarmac** surface, such as a track or a closed public street. A dirt bike, or off-road bike, is made to handle rough and bumpy terrain. Some bikes are built for races that last only seconds, while others are built for competitions that continue for weeks.

Ride like the Pros!

Sport bikes are also made for recreational activities. This kind of sport bike is made for people who enjoy riding sport bikes but do not want to compete in races. A recreational sport bike is less powerful than a high-performance sport bike and has **street-legal** features such as turning signals, headlights, and **odometers**. Dirt bikes do not have these features and are illegal to ride on the streets. Recreational sport bikes give the thrill of speed but are not equipped for racing.

Motocross racers fly through the air. Motocross courses are designed with many obstacles, including jumps, that challenge riders and keep the races exciting for spectators.

Race Across Land

There are many different types of competition for sport bikes. Grand Prix and Superbike races are held on paved tracks. Motocross and Supercross races are held on dirt courses, and Supermoto races are run on tracks of both dirt and tarmac. Drag races are between two riders who race down a quarter-mile strip of track. Ice racing is done on ice tracks, and Freestyle Motocross races allow riders to do tricks while flying through the air.

Winning Design

Sport bike racing helps engineers and designers to build better motorcycles. Many new technologies have been invented to help bikes go faster or handle better as a result of the sport. These technologies are often seen on street bikes a few years after they are first used at the racetrack. Some sport bikes, such as top-level drag racers, are so specialized that they cannot be purchased at dealerships. The technology behind these bikes is limited to the racetrack.

Bikes built for top speeds position riders so that they minimize air resistance that can slow them down.

Dirt bike competitions take racers through muddy, wet terrain. Dirt bikes are not legal to ride on the street.

Moving on Two Wheels

Motorcycles were invented in the late 1800s. The earliest motorcycles were bicycles with simple engines attached to them. Technology improved rapidly, and soon, people were racing their two-wheeled machines on streets around the world.

Bone Shakers

The first bicycles were built in the mid-1800s. These bicycles had steel frames and wooden wheels with iron rims on the outside. Many people called these bikes "bone shakers" because the hard wheels made the rider feel every bump in the road. The first motorized bicycle was made by attaching a steam engine to the bike. The engine was impractical because it burned coal for fuel, which was heavy and bulky. Nicholaus Otto invented the **four-stroke internal combustion engine** in 1876. The engine ran on gasoline, and was small enough to fit the lightweight, delicate frame of a bicycle.

Indian was a major motorcycle company in America. Indian was Harley Davidson's main competitor on the race track and the two companies battled fiercely for victories. This early version, made in 1911, won first, second, and third places at the Isle of Man Tourist Trophy that year.

A One-Track Mind

Gottlieb Daimler is credited with developing the first motorcycle in 1885. It had two wheels of similar size in the front and back and two small wheels at the sides for stability. It was made of wood and had iron-rimmed tires. The machine ran on a simple, gasoline-powered engine. Gottlieb Daimler's son Paul became the first motorcyclist when he rode his father's invention from Cannstatt, Germany, to a town six miles away. He made it, but it is said that the engine got so hot in its location under the seat that it caught on fire on the way!

Racers warm up at a Grand Prix in 1969. Both racers are riding bikes made by Italian manufacturer, Ducati.

Small & Speedy

The sport of motorcycle racing started in the early 1900s. It quickly became popular in Europe and the United States. In 1903, motorcyclists in the northeastern United States formed a club for racing called the Federation of American Motorcyclists. The club's members competed against one another in races that took place over long distances and several days. This club later turned into the modern American Motorcyclist Association (AMA), which still runs today. In 1907, the world's first motor sports racetrack, the Brooklands Motor Course, was built in England. The circular track had **banked turns** and was closed to the public. Motorsport racers quickly began breaking speed records at Brooklands because it was designed to help cars and motorcycles go as fast as possible.

7

Built for Speed

Sport bikes have hundreds of different parts under their sleek exteriors. All of the parts work together to make the bike go fast, handle well, or endure different types of terrain.

Fairing

The fairing is a shield of plastic that wraps around the handlebars of the bike. It helps the wind flow over the rider better, helping the bike go faster. It also provides some protection for the rider against flying debris.

Handlebars

The handlebars allow the rider to steer the bike. Many important controls are found on the handlebars, such as the **throttle** to increase speed, turn indicators, the front brake, and the kill switch, which turns off the engine.

Suspension

The suspension is a set of springs attached to the front and back wheels of the bike that help the bike handle better and make the rider more comfortable.

Wheels & Tires

A wheel is made of a metal rim and a rubber tire. Tires have different treads, or surfaces, for different driving surfaces. Smooth, treadless tires called racing slicks are used for dry tracks, while motocross tires have large, raised treads for maximum **traction** in dirt or mud.

Engine

Motorcycles use an internal combustion engine to create power. In the racing world, four-stroke engines are most common. This engine has four cylinders.

Seat

Bike seats are shaped differently for different sports. For instance, a motocross bike has a long seat so that the rider can change positions while racing.

Chassis

The chassis is the frame of the motorcycle. It is usually made of solid metal such as aluminum or steel. Many other parts are attached to the chassis, including the engine, seat, handlebars, fuel tank, and **gearbox**.

Transmission

The transmission system transfers power from the engine to the back wheel. The transmission has a chain, a gearbox, and a clutch. The clutch connects the engine to the gearbox. Higher gears are used for high speeds, and lower gears are used for slower speeds.

On Track

Most sport bike races are held on tracks specially designed for the sport. Racing events are usually divided into categories for different sizes of bikes. Professional races are usually part of a series in which an overall winner is decided at the end of the racing season.

A Global Sport

Motorcycle races take place all over the world. The most popular racing events are Grand Prix, Superbike, and motocross. These races take place at large stadiums that hold thousands of people. Grand Prix and Superbike are classified as road races, as they take place on paved tracks. Motocross races take place on dirt tracks with natural features, such as hills and bumps. These tracks are usually made just for motocross racing.

Series Racing

The international governing body for racing is the Fédération Internationale de Motocyclisme (FIM). It creates rules and safety standards for five types of motorcycle racing, including road racing, motocross, trials, enduro, and Speedway. The FIM also organizes World Championship series in each sport. Riders and teams compete for points in races, and at the end of the year, the rider or team with the most points is named World Champion. FIM races are international, but many countries have national race organizations as well. In the United States, the American Motorcyclist Association (AMA) organizes a National Championship series for Supercross, Superbike, and motocross.

A motocross racer kicks up dirt at an outdoor race course. Unlike Supercross, which usually takes place at indoor stadiums, motocross races include natural features and obstacles, such as trees, ditches, and hills.

Team Play

Although there are many types of motorcycle racing and each is very different, there are some parts of racing that remain the same. Professional motorcycle racers are part of a team, which is usually sponsored by one or more large companies. These companies, usually motorcycle manufacturers, give the team **salaries** for racing and pay for all of the racing costs. The team includes engineers and mechanics, who make sure the bikes are ready for the race, as well as managers and other support staff who help racers plan their schedules and arrange meetings with the media and fans.

Divisions

Racing series are usually divided into different classes based on engine sizes. Engine size is described in cubic centimeters (cc). Common size classes include 125cc, 250cc, 450 or 500cc, 750 or 800cc, and 900cc. A division may also state whether the engine must be a two-stroke or four-stroke. Basing the classes on engine size is meant to ensure that the bikes are similar in performance so the riders' skills are tested as well as the performance of their bikes.

British rider Neil Hodgson races to the finish line at a Superbike race in Germany in 2003. Hodgson, like most racers, enjoys several types of motorcycle racing, including motocross and MotoGP.

Race Day

Large motorcycle events usually take place on weekends, with the final race on Saturday or Sunday afternoons. Racers arrive days before the race in order to set up their paddock area, participate in practice rounds, and compete in qualifying races.

The Paddock

Race preparation takes place in the paddock, a large area near the racetrack. The paddock is where the teams set up tents and special trucks or trailers that hold all of the racing gear. The trucks are small-sized repair shops on wheels that travel everywhere with the race team. The bikes are tuned in the paddock, while the drivers prepare for the race ahead.

The Daytona International Speedway in Florida is a famous track where several types of racing take place, including motorcycles, pickup trucks, and stock cars.

Practice and Qualifying

In many racing series, riders must qualify to compete in the main race. The results of these races, called qualifiers, determine if they can move on to the final event of the weekend. In some types of racing, such as Superbike racing, the qualifiers and pre-race **heats** also determine the riders' starting position in the final event. The best position in most types of track-based racing is the starting position closest to the inside of the track. It is called the pole position. This puts the rider in the best position to get out in front of the pack of other racers at the beginning of the race.

Race Day

In most road races, warm-up rounds take place in the morning of race day, and the final race takes place in the afternoon. During warm-up rounds, the riders warm up their bikes and get a feel for the track's condition that day. When it is time for the final event, the riders enter the track via the **pit lane** and complete one lap of the track called a sighting lap. Next, they line up in the **starting grid**. In Grand Prix racing, the riders line up in a V-shaped pattern with the fastest qualifying rider in the pole position. The riders complete one warm-up lap and regain their positions in the grid. The start of the race is indicated when a red light at the starting gate goes out after being lit for two to five seconds.

American racer Nicky Hayden gets air during a qualifying round at the British Grand Prix.

And the Winner Is...

The rider to complete the designated number of laps the fastest wins the race. When the winning rider crosses the finish line, the track marshal waves a checkered flag to show the other racers that the race has been won. Winning riders sometimes become very famous, and are often featured in magazines or on television shows, and have thousands of fans.

Superbike racer Ben Spies celebrates his victory.

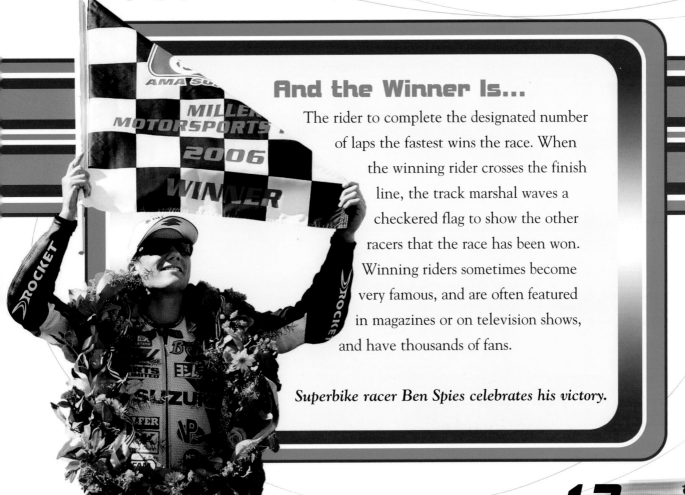

Grand Prix 3

World Championship Grand Prix racing motorcycles are technologically advanced and extremely fast. A top Grand Prix bike can reach speeds of over 186 miles per hour (300 kilometers per hour). Grand Prix motorcycles are not available to purchase for street riding.

The Great Divide

World Championship Grand Prix racing has three divisions based on engine size: 125cc, 250cc, and MotoGP (800cc). Riders only race against other riders on bikes of the same engine size. Each racing event has practices, qualifiers, and finals for each division. The finals of each division are run on the Sunday of race week, with the 125cc class first, the 250cc second, and the MotoGP class last.

MotoGP Madness

The 2007 Grand Prix series has 18 races that take place in 16 different countries. The best racers and fastest bikes compete in the MotoGP division. It is the most famous division and is the most popular with fans. At each race, riders compete fiercely to win points for the World Championship title. The average speed of motorcycles in a MotoGP race is between 96 miles per hour (155 kilometers per hour) and 112 miles per hour (180 kilometers per hour).

Italian racer Valentino Rossi takes a look at his bike and makes adjustments before a MotoGP training session.

Tracks

Grand Prix races are a distance of 59 miles (95 kilometers) to 81 miles (130 kilometers). The courses are made of tarmac and have both right and left turns and long, straight stretches. The irregular shape and tight turns in the track design are meant to control the speed of the race by forcing the rider to slow down to go into the turns. Tracks that have more straight lines are faster than tracks that have many corners.

Spanish racer Tony Elias navigates a sharp corner at the Sepang International Circuit in Malaysia, during a MotoGP race in 2005.

Speed Machines

Grand Prix motorcycles are made strictly for racing. They are not sold in stores and they are not driven on the street. They are for racetracks only. Grand Prix motorcycles are lightweight, so they can achieve high speeds. Manufacturers reduce weight by using ultra-light materials, such as **carbon fiber** or **titanium**, to built parts of the bike such as the exhaust pipe. The structure of a Grand Prix motorcycle is very important. Its body is slightly shorter than an average motorcycle and it is closer to the ground. The distance between the bike's front tire and back tire is longer than an average motorcycle to give it more stability at high speeds.

15

Superbikes

Superbikes are regular-production **sport bikes that have been modified for racing**. The bikes are not as specialized as Grand Prix bikes. Superbike races are some of the most exciting in motorsports.

Superbike Explosion

The first Superbikes were built in the 1970s, when Japanese manufacturers, including Honda and Suzuki, created stylish new motorcycles such as the Honda CB 750 and the Suzuki GS 550. These bikes were inexpensive but had high performance and a racing-influenced appearance. The look and power of these bikes made them very popular among motorcycle enthusiasts.

Superbike is Born

The AMA was the first organization to introduce a Superbike racing series in 1976. Motorcycle companies were excited by the series because it gave them the opportunity to show off brand new models to the public. Since Superbikes could be purchased in dealerships, it was an effective sales strategy. In 1988, the FIM created a Superbike World Championship series and international participation in the sport grew.

A Supersport bike awaits the attention of mechanics in the pit.

Support Classes

The AMA has several divisions in its Superbike series. These divisions, called support classes, are for bikes that are less powerful, and often raced by less experienced riders. These classes include Supersport, Superstock, and Formula Xtreme. Riders from these classes often move up to the Superbike Championship series after riding in the support classes for several years. All support class races are a distance of 37 miles (60 kilometers). Superstock engines can range from 745cc to 1000cc. Formula Xtreme bikes have the largest-sized engines in the AMA series, ranging from 550cc to 1350cc.

Two Supersport racers compete at the Brands Hatch circuit in England.

Super Style

In Superbike racing, there are very strict rules about what parts of the bike can be enhanced. The engines are made more powerful with small modifications. Superbikes have stiffer suspensions so that they handle better at high speeds. Stiff suspensions help bikes react faster as riders adjust their position on the bike. This allows the rider to maintain control. The seat is located toward the back of the bike, and the handlebars are set low, placing riders in a forward position with their legs slightly behind them. This position makes the rider and the motorcycle more **aerodynamic** so that air flows over the rider more easily. In dry conditions, superbikes use racing slicks. In wet conditions, the bikes are equipped with tires with tread, but this slows down the bikes because the tire creates more **friction** with the ground.

Motocross

3

Motocross racing is done on outdoor dirt tracks or trails. Motocross bikes are built for handling rough, bumpy terrain. Motocross racing is popular all over the world.

Moto Worldwide

The American Motorcyclist Association (AMA) runs a national motocross race series in the United States. Similar series take place in other countries, such as Great Britain, Canada, Spain, France, New Zealand, and Russia. The Fédération Internationale de Motocyclisme (FIM) organizes the World Championship series of motocross racing. Races in this series are held all over the world.

On Course

Motocross races take place on dirt courses. Courses are usually between half a mile and two miles long. They often include many tight turns to test the rider's ability to maintain control while speeding around corners. Motorcycles often skid out to the side around the tight corners on a motocross track and riders have to put one of their feet down to keep their bikes from tipping over. **Obstacles** on the course include hand-built jumps, hills, and series of bumps called washboards. Motocross courses are usually built in the country because they require a lot of space.

A motocross rider braces himself as he makes a sharp turn. Motocross racing requires a lot of strength and energy. Riders have to use their arms and legs to keep control of the bikes as they navigate short, tight corners and fly over huge jumps.

The Dirt Flies!

There are two divisions in the AMA Motocross series: 250cc and 450cc. A motocross race consists of two rounds of racing, called motos. Points are awarded to each rider based on their finishing position. The rider who wins the most points after the two motos is the overall winner of the race. Each moto is 30 minutes long plus two laps. Up to 40 racers can compete at once. The racers all start at the same time and they race around the course until the flag is waved showing that 30 minutes is up. This tells the riders there are two laps left. The winner of the race is the rider who crosses the finish line first after finishing their final two laps.

Motocross Features

One of the most important components of a motocross bike is its suspension. The suspension is a system of springs that absorb bumps and jumps as the bike travels over the ground. The suspension is located in the **front forks** of the bike and in the back just behind the engine. Other motocross-specific features include mudguards over the tires and in front of the hand grips to protect the bike and the rider from mud spray. The seat is much longer than a regular bike to allow the rider to change positions when going over bumps and jumps. Motocross bikes are not street-legal in many countries, so they do not have features such as headlights and turn indicators.

Supercross

Supercross is similar to motocross racing, but the races are held on indoor courses at arenas or stadiums. Sometimes the races are held at an outdoor venue, such as the inner oval of the Daytona Superspeedway, a famous racetrack in Florida. The races are almost the same as motocross races, but often include more jumps to impress the fans. Supercross racing is very popular in the United States.

Freestyle Motocross riders risk their lives with dangerous stunts. Injuries are common, and some riders have died.

Off-Track Extreme

Track-based racing is just not enough for some motorcycle riders. They want to push their bikes to the extreme. From jumping a motorcycle over 100 feet in the air while letting go of the handles, to racing across the desert for close to a month, these riders take off-track racing to a whole new level.

Freestyle Motocross

Freestyle Motocross, or FMX as it is commonly called, is a type of motocross that is focused on jumps, tricks, and stunts. There are two kinds of FMX. The first, commonly called a Big Air competition, is performed on two metal ramps. Riders race down one ramp and use their speed to launch off another. They fly through the air and do a trick in mid-air. Riders' tricks are judged on a scale of 1 to 100, with 100 being a perfect jump. The other kind of FMX is called Freestyle Motocross. Riders navigate a dirt course filled with jumps, on which riders perform tricks. Two of the most impressive tricks are the Backflip and the Double Backflip. In this trick, riders flip their bikes over backwards once or twice while airborne. FMX is very dangerous and serious injuries, resulting in death, can occur.

Supermoto

Supermoto is a combination of Superbike racing and motocross racing. A Supermoto course is set up to alternate between a pavement course and a dirt-track motocross-style course. The fastest rider to the end of the course wins each race. The bikes used are motocross-style bikes with road-racing wheels and slick, or slightly grooved, tires.

FMX riders practice their tricks by launching off ramps and into pits filled with foam.

Enduro Racing

Enduro races are some of the toughest races in the world. The goal of an enduro race is to complete a specific distance in a set amount of time. Racers are penalized for going over or under the set time. Enduro races can last up to 24 hours. They are raced in teams, with two or three riders each riding a different stage of the course. Races take place on outdoor courses over large distances. Riders race to checkpoints, or stops, on the course, where their time is recorded. Riders also refuel and repair their bikes at checkpoints. If a bike breaks down on the course, riders must push their bike to the next checkpoint. The bikes used for enduro racing are motocross-style bikes with street-legal features such as headlights and turning signals, because enduro courses sometimes cover public roads. The main goal of an enduro race is to meet the time allotted and this makes it different than a long-distance rally race, which is a long-distance race to get to the finish first.

Desert Racing

The most famous desert race is the Dakar Rally, formerly called the Paris Dakar Rally. It is a three-week distance rally race from Europe to Dakar, Senegal, on the west coast of Africa. Cars, trucks, and motorcycles are all allowed to participate in the race. The Dakar Rally covers thousands of miles and routes are often up to 10,000 miles (16,093 km) long. The race is conducted in stages, or mini-races, and the driver with the fastest overall time wins. Riders race as individuals but rely on a team of mechanics, engineers, and supporters to help them with refueling and maintaining their vehicles every day. The Dakar Rally is an extremely tough race. Riders must find their own way and are not allowed to use **global positioning systems** (GPS) to help plot their course.

Richard Sainct of France racing in the Dakar Rally in 2004. Sainct died later that year during the Rally de Pharaon, or Pharaoh's Rally, in Egypt.

Drag Racing

Drag racing motorcycles are designed for top speed in short bursts. Drag racing is a sport where two bikes race side by side on a quarter-mile stretch of track. The first rider to cross the finish line wins the race. Drag racing bikes are long, low to the ground, and very fast.

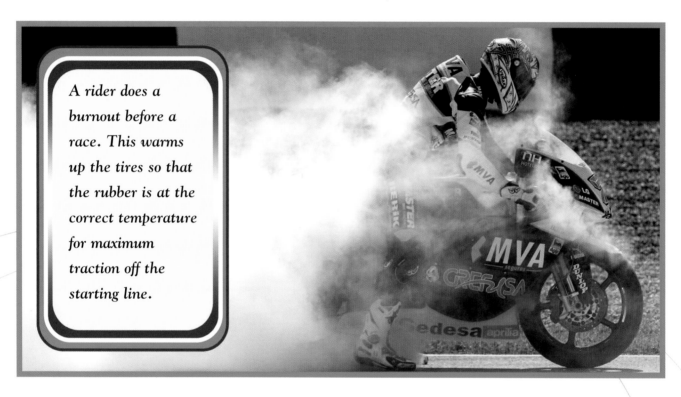

A rider does a burnout before a race. This warms up the tires so that the rubber is at the correct temperature for maximum traction off the starting line.

A Need for Speed

The first drag races were informal races between two motorcyclists. These races, which usually took place on abandoned roads, were very dangerous and illegal. The AMA created a drag racing series to provide a safer setting for drag races. The AMA/Prostar series is the national series for drag racing in the U.S. There are over 10 divisions in the series, based on different types of motorcycles, engine size, and fuel. The Top Fuel division is for custom-made motorcycles that reach up to 200 mph (322 km/h).

Off The Line

The goal of drag racing is to reach the fastest speed in the shortest amount of time. Races are run in heats, with the slower rider of each race being **eliminated**. The winner of the final race is declared overall champion. Before each race, riders are called to a special area behind the starting line. Here they do a burnout, where they keep the bike in one place while spinning the back wheel at top speed. The riders then wait for the start signal. A good start sends the rider flying down the track to the finish line at top speed.

(right) Drag racers are positioned so far forward that they are almost lying down on their bikes. This minimizes wind resistance, which cuts speed.

Power and Speed

Professional drag racing motorcycles are designed to produce maximum power with a minimum amount of weight. The engines work so hard during a race that they do not usually last for more than one race. The back tire is one of the most important parts of the bike. It is responsible for transferring all the power from the engine to the racetrack. The back tire is much larger than the front tire, and is very wide so that it has more surface for starting-line traction. Behind the tire of a drag racer is a wheelie bar. The bar is needed to prevent the bike from tipping over backwards when the bikes launch off the starting line.

Fueled for Speed

Instead of gasoline, some motorcycles in the Top Fuel division are fueled by a mixture of nitromethane and methanol. Others are powered by nitrous oxide, a gas. These substances create more engine power because they burn more efficiently.

A drag racer roars off the starting line in a gust of fuel vapors and burnt rubber.

Tourist Trophy

The Isle of Man Tourist Trophy (TT) motorcycle race was first run in 1907. It takes place on the Isle of Man, an island in the British Isles. The race takes place on public streets that are closed for the event. Thousands of people come to watch the race every year.

The Race

The Isle of Man TT is one of the most famous and challenging motorcycle races in the world. The race course has changed several times since its early days, but it has always taken place on public roads. The current course used for the race is called the Snaefell Mountain Course. It starts in the island's capital city of Douglas, and brings riders through villages and countryside. The course is 37 miles (60 kilometers) long and each rider does six laps, for a total distance of over 226 miles (364 kilometers). There are over 200 bends in the course and many of them are very tight. Riders race through the course at top speed. The most recent record set for speed was in 2006, when John McGuiness of England achieved an average lap time of 129 miles per hour (208 kilometers per hour).

Danger Zone

The Isle of Man TT is one of the most dangerous races in the world. The tight turns and high speeds are a dangerous combination. Many riders have died in the race in its 100-year history. It is dangerous for the fans as well. Spectators line the sides of the course to watch the action and are only protected by fences and bales of straw that are set out in case of a crash. The TT was part of the FIM Grand Prix World Championship series until 1980. The status was removed after the top riders in the world refused to ride in the TT because they felt it was too dangerous.

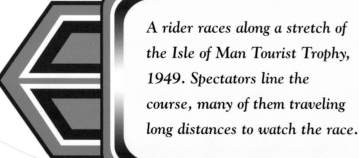

A rider races along a stretch of the Isle of Man Tourist Trophy, 1949. Spectators line the course, many of them traveling long distances to watch the race.

TT Machines

The racing divisions for the TT are the same as those used for FIM-sanctioned World Championship Superbike racing, and the bikes raced fall under the same regulations. The TT has five divisions for different motorcycles, including TT Superbike, TT Superstock, Supersport Junior TT, TT Senior, and Sidecar TT. Sidecars are one-wheeled pods that are attached to the side of a motorcycle for an extra passenger. Each division is further divided into engine classes. For example, the Superbike category has three engine formats allowed from 750cc to 1000cc with two, three, or four cylinders. The different divisions of motorcycles race on different days. Each rider must qualify for the race in timed practice rounds before entering the final race.

Race teams line up at the starting line of a classic motorcycle sidecar race at Brands Hatch, England, in 1965.

The Race Today

The Tourist Trophy is very popular. It celebrates its 100th anniversary in 2007. The race now includes a two-week festival with parades, races, and special events. Over 40,000 people arrive at the island every year to see the race. They come to watch and maybe even meet professional riders who are out and part of the crowds when they are not racing. There is even an event in which spectators can participate called Mad Sunday, where fans can ride their own motorcycles around the TT course!

Sidecar Racing

Sidecar racing is a division in the Isle of Man TT. A sidecar is a small car that looks like a bobsleigh and is attached to the side of a motorcycle. The sidecar has its own engine and driver. The driver of the motorcycle and the driver of the sidecar must work together to drive. The sidecar driver helps steer by using body weight to turn corners and to speed up and slow down the bike.

Speedway Racing

Speedway motorcycles do not have brakes or suspensions, and they have only one gear. They race around the track at high speeds and thrill crowds with their exciting and dangerous performance.

Ice racing takes place on ice instead of shale. Some riders cover their knees with pieces of old tires to protect their legs from hitting the ice when they take corners. Ice racing is most popular in cold climates, such as Eastern Europe and Scandinavia.

Around and Around

Speedway racing is held on quarter-mile long oval tracks. Riders race around the track in a counter-clockwise direction and the first person, or team, to complete four laps wins the race or heat. Speedway races are run as individual or team events, in which pairs of riders compete against one another. Teams often represent their home countries. Speedway racing was first invented in the United States in the early 1900s, but it quickly became very popular in Australia. It is now a global sport and is especially popular in Britain, Poland, and Sweden.

Nighttime Excitement

Some Speedway races are run at night under lights. Races are run in heats, and there are as many as 20 heats per night. Each heat has four riders who complete four laps. In the FIM Speedway World Championship Grand Prix racing series, riders or teams compete for points. Points are determined by finishing position. The first-place rider gets three points, the second place rider gets two pionts, and the third place rider gets one point. The last rider is eliminated.

Powerslides

Speedway racing tracks are made of shale, or very thin pieces of rock. This is because the bikes have no brakes and the riders have to powerslide, or swing the back of the bike out around a corner, to slow down for turns. The shale surface helps the riders keep control of the bike because it shifts with the bike and prevents it from skidding out in a corner. The sides of the track are lined with fences to protect the crowds in case of a crash.

Speedway Machines

Speedway motorcycles are basic machines that have not changed much since the mid-1900s. Their technology is simple and the skill of the rider is more important than the power of the bike. Speedway bikes have 500cc, single-cylinder, four-stroke engines that are fueled by methanol, an alternative fuel to gasoline. Methanol creates a denser mix of air and fuel in the engine's cylinder, which creates more power. The bikes' front forks are steeply angled in comparison to a regular motorcycle so that the bike is more stable as it races around corners at high speeds.

(left) The tires of ice racing motorcycles are fitted with metal spikes so that they grip the ice.

(below) Speedway races cover a distance of about 1 mile (1.6 kilometers).

Equipment

3

Motorcycle racing is a very dangerous sport. Riders have special equipment to protect themselves from injury and weather. They wear protective suits, as well as helmets, gloves, and boots.

Helmet

The helmet is the most important piece of equipment a motorcyclist wears. Helmets have a hard plastic outer shell and a softer inner layer of foam and fabric. The inner foam is made of **expanded polystyrene**. The foam inside is often covered by fabric so the interior of the helmet is more comfortable against the rider's head. The hard outer shell of the helmet is designed to help protect the rider's head from hard objects that might pierce the rider's head in a crash. Sport bike racers wear full-face helmets that cover their entire heads down to the top of their necks. A section in the front covers their chins. A shield for the face is pulled down while riding. This helps protect the rider's face from rain and insects.

Helmets are the most important piece of equipment because they help protect riders from brain injury in the event of a crash. Brain injuries can lead to concussions, memory loss, or death.

Hector Barbera is dragged across the track to scuff his new leathers before a race. Many racers share this superstition.

(below) Motocross boots have extra protection on the shins to guard riders' legs from the rugged terrain.

Racing Suits

A full racing suit includes a one-piece suit made of leather or fabric, special boots, gloves, and protective body armor that is built into the suit or worn underneath it. Leather is the most common material used to make motorcycle suits. MotoGP racers and Superbike racers wear one-piece leather suits. Motocross riders and some recreational riders wear suits of **synthetic** fabrics such as Cordura, a special **abrasion-resistant** fabric. Racing suits have built-in armor, made out of a strong synthetic material such as **Kevlar**, to protect riders in case of falls or accidents. Superbike and MotoGP riders wear special knee pads to protect them when they turn corners and one of their knees drag. Other armor is located over the rider's elbows, torso, hips, and shoulders. Motocross riders wear upper body armor vests under their racing jerseys, and have padding built into the knees and seats of their pants.

Boots

Motorcyclists wear calf-high boots with a small heel for riding. The heel helps the rider grip the foot **pegs** of the bike. Boots also provide protection for the lower leg from the hot exhaust pipe of the bike. Superbike and MotoGP racers wear lightweight boots made out of special fabric, leather, and plastics. They have no exterior buckles and are reinforced with hard plastic or steel on the outside of the boot in case the rider's leg touches the ground while turning a corner.

Behind the Machines

Sport bike companies constantly strive to build sleeker, faster, more powerful motorcycles. Each new technological improvement sparks a race between the companies to top each other, and this has helped make motorcycle sport so exciting.

Honda

Japanese manufacturer Honda has been a leader in sport bike development since the 1960s. An engineer named Soichiro Honda started making basic motorcycles in the mid-1940s. Honda was a former race car driver, and he made it his goal to win the Isle of Man Tourist Trophy race with his motorcycle team. He achieved his goal in the early 1960s and soon after, Honda became the biggest motorcycle manufacturing company in the world. Since then, the brand has achieved many racing victories. Honda makes motorcycles for motocross and off-track racing, MotoGP, Superbike racing and more. The company also makes a wide range of recreational motorcycles.

Yamaha

The Yamaha Motor Company made its first motorcycle in 1955. The company, founded by Torakusu Yamaha in 1887, originally made musical instruments. Yamaha's first bike was called the YA-1. It was chestnut-red, and was nicknamed the *aka-tombo*, a Japanese word for red dragonfly. The YA-1 won its very first race in 1955. Today, Yamaha makes motorcycles for all types of racing and recreation.

Soichiro Honda (1906 - 1991), founder of the Honda Motor Company, fastens his helmet while waiting for his hot air balloon to inflate in Gstaad, Switzerland. Honda was a risk taker who also raced cars early in his life.

Suzuki

Suzuki is one of the top three motorcycle manufacturers in Japan, alongside Honda and Yamaha. Suzuki was originally called Suzuki Loom Works and it made looms, machines that make fabric. Suzuki's first effort at making a motorcycle was in 1952. The Power Free was a bicycle with an engine and pedals that could be used to assist the engine's performance. Today Suzuki is a major manufacturer and it makes almost every type of racing motorcycle. Suzkui's motocross and Supercross motorcycles are especially popular.

Ducati

Ducati is an Italian sport bike manufacturer. The Ducati family founded the company in Bologna, Italy in 1926. They originally made parts for radios, but **World War II** left the Ducati factories in ruins. After the war, the family started making motorcycles. Two motorcycle magazine enthusiasts, a lawyer Aldo Farinelli and his brother, an engineer Enzo Furio, designed the first Ducati bike. It was called the Cucciolo and it had a two-speed gearbox and room to carry two passengers. The Cucciolo was fuel efficient, and became known as an endurance bike.

Ducati specializes in Superbikes and MotoGP bikes, as well as recreational motorcycles.

Glossary

abrasion-resistant Material that is difficult to tear

aerodynamic The ability to cut through the wind

banked turns Corners on a track that are elevated on one side, to help vehicles make turns safely

carbon fiber A very strong substance

concussion A brain injury that results from bruising of the brain

eliminated Removed from competition

expanded polystyrene Firm, lightweight material

four-stroke An engine that creates power in four stages: intake, compression, power, and exhaust

friction Resistance between two surfaces

front forks The part of the motorcycle that holds the front wheel on and allows steering

gearbox A device that houses gears of an engine

global positioning system A navigational system

heats Rounds of races before the main event

internal combustion engine An engine that creates power by burning fuel

Kevlar A strong synthetic material

obstacles Objects placed on a race track to challenge racers

odometers Devices that show the speed of a bike

pegs Places for motorcyclists to put their feet

pit lane The part of the track where riders go for repairs or refueling during a race

regular-production Made in a factory and sold in dealerships to the public

salaries Payment over the course of a year

starting grid The positioning of all racers at the beginning of a race

street-legal Having the appropriate equipment for riding on the street

synthetic Artificial or unnatural materials

tarmac A hard, paved surface

throttle A device that controls flow of fuel to the engine for acceleration or deceleration of a bike

titanium A light, hard, silver-colored metal

touring bikes Motorcycles that are built for long-distance traveling

traction The grip of a tire on a surface

tread Bumps and grooves in a tire that help it grip the road

World War II A global conflict fought from 1939 to 1945.

Index